Helen Orme taught as a Special Needs Co-ordinator in a large comprehensive school. At the last count she had written around 40 books, many for reluctant readers.

Helen runs writing workshops for children and courses for teachers in both primary and secondary schools.

Stalker

Helen Orme

Rans☾m

Stalker

by Helen Orme
Illustrated by Cathy Brett
Cover by Anna Torborg

Published by Ransom Publishing Ltd.
Rose Cottage, Howe Hill, Watlington, Oxon. OX49 5HB
www.ransom.co.uk

ISBN   978 184167 595 4
First published in 2007

Meet the Sisters ...

Siti and her friends are really close. So close she calls them her Sisters. They've been mates for ever, and most of the time they are closer than her real family.

Siti is the leader – the one who always knows what to do – but Kelly, Lu, Donna and Rachel have their own lives to lead as well.

Still, there's no one you can talk to, no one you can rely on, like your best mates. Right?

1

Not fair

"It's not fair," said Kelly. "Everybody else is allowed."

"I don't care," said her mum.

Kelly glared at her mum. It wasn't fair. She was never allowed to come home when she wanted. Someone always had to come and pick her up.

When it was her brother Jamie it wasn't too bad, but when it was her mum – well, who wants their mum waiting for them all the time?

"It's only round the corner," she said, trying again. "And the others will come most of the way with me."

Her mum was getting fed up. "I'll think about it," she said. "Maybe."

Kelly went up to her room to call her friends.

She rang Siti first. They started to make plans for the evening. There was a Halloween Fair near the school. It was Friday night and everybody was going to be there.

Kelly really wanted to go, but she didn't want her mum coming to find her at the end of the evening.

She went downstairs again.

"Well?" she said. "Can I go? Please, please, pretty please."

Mum sighed. "All right," she said. "But …"

Before she could finish Kelly grabbed her and started dancing round the room.

"But you MUST be home by 10 o'clock. And DON'T walk home alone."

2

The little ones

Siti and Lu came to get Kelly at 7 o'clock.

"We're meeting the others at the park," said Siti. "My mum and dad are going to be there!" She pulled a face. "They're taking the little ones."

Siti's oldest brother, Daudi, was only two years younger than she was, but she always called her brothers and sister 'the little ones'. It really wound Daudi up.

"Doesn't matter," shrugged Lu. "There will be loads of people there – we can keep well out of their way!"

"Bye, mum!" called Kelly, as they went out of the door.

"Bye Mrs Jonson," called Siti and Lu.

It took them about twenty minutes to walk to the park. Donna and Rachel were waiting for them.

"Where have you been?" asked Donna. "Look, Gary and his mates are over there."

Gary, Simon and Billy were in the same class as the girls.

Kelly fancied Gary like mad. She thought he liked her and she knew he hadn't got a girlfriend, but she was too shy to make the first move.

The rest of Gary's gang were great too, so the girls didn't mind helping Kelly get herself noticed.

They moved over to get nearer to the boys. Siti started talking to Simon.

Kelly moved so she could be nearer Gary, and was rewarded with a cheeky grin.

"Come on the ghost train with us?" he said.

"O.K."

"I don't want to," said Siti. "I want to go and get a toffee apple."

"I'll come with you," said Rachel. "I don't like ghost trains!"

3

Little pest

"Good move," said Rachel. "That gives Kelly a chance to get off with Gary."

"That's what I thought," said Siti. "Come on – what shall we do while we wait?"

"Let's get that toffee apple – then we can decide."

They went off to the stall selling toffee apples. Siti had just got hers when a hand came from behind and grabbed it.

You little pest!" she said, turning to grab Daudi, but he was off into the crowd before she could reach him.

"I'll tell mum!" she shouted, but he just kept running.

4

Egged!

Daudi was getting to be a real pest. He knew that the girls didn't want him, but he wouldn't leave them alone.

Wherever they went, whatever they did, he was following them.

He had got hold of a Halloween mask from somewhere and kept jumping out and trying to scare them.

Siti had even gone to find her mum.

"It's no good," she said when she came back. "Mum says she doesn't see what our problem is and anyway they'll be going soon. She's no help at all."

"It's so embarrassing," said Kelly. She was cross because Gary, Simon and Billy had gone off again.

"Oh stop fussing," said Donna. "Come on – let's go on that flying thing – he can't follow us there."

"Don't want to," said Kelly. "I'll stay down here and wait for you."

Donna was getting fed up with Kelly. She dragged Rachel over to the ride.

"Will you be O.K.?" asked Siti.

" 'Course I will," snapped Kelly. She gave Siti a push. "I'll wait over by the bumper cars."

Kelly looked towards the bumper cars. She could see Gary over there.

She poked Siti and nodded.

"See you soon then," she said as they went off.

Kelly waved at them and then turned away. She began to walk towards the bumper cars. There was no sign of Gary now.

She looked round the corner. No sign of the boys!

She turned back again and suddenly there was a yell and she felt something slimy on her head. Next a cloud of flour covered her hair.

She heard laughter. It was that stupid Daudi and a couple of his friends.

"Got you! Got you!"

"You stupid brats! I'm going to tell your mum, Daudi."

Kelly wiped her hands through her hair. Egg! Ugh!

She was nearly crying now. It had been a foul evening so far. She made up her mind. She was going home.

5

'I'm going home'

She headed back towards the Sisters. They were just getting off the ride when she got to them.

"Your stupid brother did this!" she said to Siti. "Look at me! I'm not staying any longer. I'm fed up with it all. I'm going home."

"We can't go yet," said Rachel. "It's only half nine. The fun hasn't started yet."

"No one said you had to come with me."

"Your mum did," said Siti.

"I know. But that was when she thought I'd be later. You stay. I'll see you tomorrow."

She turned and walked off.

Siti looked at the others. "We ought to go with her, really," she said.

"She'll be fine," said Lu. "Look – there's Simon waving to us."

Kelly was so cross. She planned what she would do to Daudi next time she saw him.

The roads were quiet. Everybody had gone to the fair. They were all enjoying themselves. They were all having fun.

It was getting really cold now. She hadn't felt cold when she was with the Sisters, but she did now. She wished she'd worn jeans instead of her shortest skirt. It was all Gary's fault. Why did she bother?

It had got foggy. The street lights were dimmed and the light didn't seem to reach as far.

She heard a noise.

A quiet noise. Footsteps.

6

Footsteps

She slowed down a bit – the quiet
footsteps slowed down too. She looked over
her shoulder, but whoever it was had ducked
away down an alley.

What should she do? Should she go back?
But she was halfway home. Anyway there
was no one there now.

She was being stupid, but she couldn't
help thinking of all the things her mum had
said in the past.

No! Mum just said those things to scare her. Nothing was going to happen. She would be home soon.

She carried on walking. She tried to be quiet so she could listen for noises behind her. Should she run? She was no good at running. If she ran she'd get all out of breath and she wouldn't be able to fight.

Fight! Who was she kidding? She couldn't fight!

Maybe she'd got something to hit him with.

She'd got that comb in her bag – it had a pointy end.

But if she stopped to get it out he might catch up.

"Stupid, stupid, stupid," she thought to herself. "There's NO ONE there."

She started to walk more quickly. There was someone coming towards her. It was O.K. – just some guy with a pizza box. He barely glanced at her as he went past.

"I could yell for help," she thought "If ..."

"No – stop right there," she told herself. "Ten more minutes, that's all."

She carried on down the street. No more noises. She was nearly home. She was going to be O.K.

Then she heard the footsteps again. Louder this time. Running. And the noise of someone breathing heavily.

She was so close, so close now. The end of
her street. She could see her own front door.
The lights were on. Mum was home.

She stopped outside the door. The
footsteps stopped too.

Her key was in her pocket. There – she
was inside. She was safe.

"Hello love, you're early," called her mum from the living room. "Come and tell me all about it."

Kelly took a deep breath. No way was she going to tell mum. NO WAY.

"In a minute – just got to go to the bathroom." She ran up the stairs to the safety of her bedroom.

The front door banged again. He'd followed her. He was in the house!

Then she heard mum again.

"Hi, Jamie. How'd it go?"

The sitting room door closed and she flopped back on her bed. No more walking home alone, she decided. Not ever.

Downstairs Jamie was telling mum how it had gone.

"I followed her all the way home, mum. It wasn't her fault she was by herself – but she was fine."

"No – she never knew I was there."